T0207568

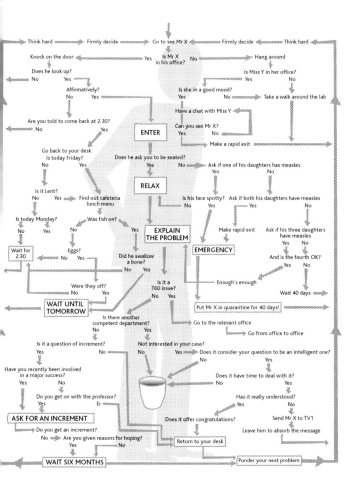

# THE ART AND CRAFT OF APPROACHING YOUR HEAD OF DEPARTMENT TO SUBMIT A REQUEST FOR A RAISE

Georges Perec (1936–82) won the Prix Renaudot in 1965 for his first novel *Things: A Story of the Sixties*, and went on to exercise his unrivalled mastery of language in almost every imaginable kind of writing, from the apparently trivial to the deeply personal. He composed acrostics, anagrams, autobiography, criticism, crosswords, descriptions of dreams, film scripts, heterograms, lipograms, memories, palindromes, plays, poetry, radio plays, recipes, riddles, stories short and long, travel notes, univocalics, and, of course, novels. *Life A User's Manual*, which draws on many of Perec's other works, appeared in 1978 after nine years in the making and was acclaimed a masterpiece to put beside Joyce's *Ulysses*. It won the Prix Médicis and established Perec's international reputation.

David Bellos, the translator, is Professor of French and Comparative Literature and Director of the Program in Translation and Intercultural Communication at Princeton University.

In 2005 David Bellos was awarded the Man Booker International Translator's Prize for his many translations of the novels of the distinguished Albanian writer Ismail Kadare. He is the author of several works on Balzac, the prize-winning biography *Georges Perec: A Life in Words*, and a biography of Romain Gary, published in 2010.

ALSO BY GEORGES PEREC

# georges
# perec

## the art and craft
### of approaching your
### head of department
### to submit a request
## for a raise

TRANSLATED FROM THE FRENCH BY
David Bellos

**V**

**VERSO**

London • New York

This paperback edition published by Verso 2016
English translation first published in the US
by Verso 2011
Translation © David Bellos 2011, 2016
First published in book form as *L'art et la manière
d'aborder son chef de service pour lui demander une
augmentation*
© Hachette Littératures 2008
This text was published for the first time in December
1968, in number 4 of the journal *Enseignement
programmé* (Hachette / Dunod)

Flow chart © ML Design, based on a design
by Jacques Perriaud

1 3 5 7 9 10 8 6 4 2

**Verso**
UK: 6 Meard Street, London W1F 0EG
US: 388 Atlantic Ave, Brooklyn, NY 11217
versobooks.com

Verso is the imprint of New Left Books

ISBN-13: 978-1-78478-656-4
ISBN-13: 978-1-98478-657-1 (US EBK)

**Library of Congress Cataloging-in-Publication Data**
A catalog record for this book is available from the Library of
Congress

Typeset by Hewer Text UK Ltd, Edinburgh
Printed in the United States

# Contents

# Introduction

Forty years ago there was no Windows, Web, or email; there were no laptops and the Mac Classic had not been invented. But there were computers – huge machines in secure, air-conditioned vaults, powered by sizeable electricity substations and maintained by teams of men in white coats known as boffins. Such electronic monsters were used to crunch numbers for NASA and the nuclear deterrent by mathematicians, physicists, aeronautical engineers and astronomers. But some far-sighted minds wondered if these daunting machines could also be used, somehow or other, in the creative arts. Around 1968, a French computer company set itself the challenge of finding artists willing to have a go at using the machines that it made. By serendipity more than careful planning, the challenge ended up on the desk of a little-known writer called Georges Perec. The unclassifiable entity called *the art and craft of approaching your head of department to submit a request for a raise* is the unexpected, comical and moving outcome of an unlikely encounter.[*]

The initial idea came from Jacques Perriaud at the Computing Service of the Humanities Research Centre in Paris. To challenge a writer to use a computer's basic mode of operation as a writing device, he sketched out the procedure that an employee would need to follow to obtain an increase in pay in some large organisation. Then he broke it down into its

[*] The US edition of this book has the title *The Art of Asking Your Boss for a Raise* on the cover.

individual steps and laid the procedure out as an algorithm, or flow-chart. As is well-known to all who work for big firms or government departments, such procedures do not always succeed on their first iteration. Perriaud's flow-chart includes ample opportunities for recursion, or going back to square one.

Georges Perec accepted the challenge to write as a computer functions, but characteristically, he seems to have negotiated a number of changes to the ground-plan before he started. At all events, the flow-chart that he used, reproduced on the endpapers to this book, has comical details like a wastepaper bin and strange loops that may or may not have come from the mind of the original designer.

Georges Perec, born 7 March 1936, had recently been co-opted to full membership of a rather special group that called itself Oulipo, short for *Ouvroir de littérature potentielle,* or 'Workshop for Potential Literature'. It was founded fifty years ago, in 1960, by the writer Raymond Queneau and the mathematician François Le Lionnais with the purpose of exploring the possible uses of mathematics and formal modes of thought in the production of new literature. Oulipo sought to invent new kinds of rules for literary composition, and also to explore the use of now-forgotten forms in the literatures of the past. Perhaps the most famous of these ancient devices – famous nowadays almost exclusively because of the work of Georges Perec – is the lipogram, which involves writing in a restricted set of characters, that is to say, without one or more letters of the alphabet. But the idea of concocting a story that proceeds by a set of programmed choices between different out-turns at each juncture was also a subject of some interest. Vaguely referred to as 'matrix literature', the idea, similar to the structure of 'Tracker Books' for children, gave rise to a short but also very long experiment by Raymond Queneau called *Un Conte à Votre Façon*, or 'A Story As You Like It', which has now been put on the Web in English translation. Each sentence is followed by a question with two possible answers. The reader chooses one of the answers, and goes on to the appropriately numbered sentence. If you make the other choice, the text directs you to a different sentence. In that way, from a small set of cunningly designed propositions an infinitely large set of stories can be made.

Perec had heard about this exercise but chose to deal quite differently with the mock-algorithm he had in front of him. Instead of leaving the reader to navigate around a labyrinth of yes/no questions and answers as Queneau had done, he chose to write out *in extenso* the progress of an imaginary computer-mind as it iterates a set of choices in pseudo-real time. He also chose to simulate the speed and tireless repetitiveness of a computer program by abandoning all forms of punctuation as well as the distinction between upper- and lower-case letters. The result is an almost unreadable fifty-page text that looks like (but actually is not) a single, breathless sentence.

*the art and craft of approaching your head of department to submit a request for a raise* was first published in an academic review devoted to what was then called Programmed Learning, or computer-assisted education, where it lay dormant for over forty years. However, around the time of its first publication, Perec was asked by his German translator, Eugen Helmle, if he might come up with something suitable for broadcast on radio. He did: an amazing though quite different simulation of a computer taking a poem by Goethe to pieces, first broadcast in German as *Die Maschine* (an English translation has appeared in *The Review of Contemporary Fiction*, XXIX, 1, 2009). The huge success of this irreverent radio play prompted requests for more such material, and Perec turned back to his other 'computer' exercise, *the art and craft . . .* for inspiration. He saw that the very design of the exercise relied on a set of six distinct and identifiable operators that could be ascribed to different voices: the situation ('you go to see your head'); the question ('is he? . . .'); the positive hypothesis ('if he is . . .'); the negative hypothesis ('if he isn't . . .'); the decider ('he isn't . . .'); and the outcome ('so off you go . . .'). With the help of Helmle, who had a lot of radio experience, Perec produced a text that was broadcast as *Wucherungen* (The Raise) on Saarland Radio in November 1969. The original French text was then picked up by Marcel Cuvelier – the long-standing director of the plays of Eugène Ionesco at the Théâtre de la Huchette, in which he also acted – as an ideal script for a non-figurative, almost static, and utterly hilarious stage production. Georges

Perec finally added *playwright* to the list of literary professions he had mastered.

The dramatic version had a successful run in Paris in 1970 but its triumph came in 1972, once again in German translation, as *Die Gehaltserhöhung*, in productions that were more agit-prop than absurdist, in Munich, Münster and Wiesbaden. The play is now often performed in France by amateur and professional companies and has been translated into Italian and Swedish and probably other languages too, but it has never been staged in English.

In the 'prose' as in the 'radio' version of this simulation of a flow-chart in action Perec pursues the exhilarating potential of repetitiveness and recursion, but he does not stick to the mindless monotony that a real computer would experience (if it could be said to experience anything at all). Enthralled as he is by writing with rules and with the exhaustive completion of self-devised schemes and grids,

• xiv •

Perec seeks in these 'logic' texts as in all his works to communicate a human experience of the world. Each of the standard formulas he devised to represent the fixed steps in the recursive procedure is repeated often enough with precision to make the variations that he introduces at some stage both comic and significant. As time goes on, the supplicant for a raise grows older; the world around him changes ever so slightly; and the story – for there *is* a story buried inside – speaks to us in the end of entropy and human mortality.

Perec reused the material of *the art and craft* one last time in Chapter 98 of *Life A User's Manual*, where he gives the topic of obtaining a raise in pay a different and more novelistic turn. Even so, the character of Maurice Réol is distinctly familiar to anyone who has read, heard or seen any one of the many versions of the project whose true original is translated here.

Translating a text which is close to being

unreadable in the original is a paradoxical but not a particularly difficult task, since ordinary readability is hardly an issue. Assuming a willing explorer of this strange and wonderful corner of the universe of Georges Perec, I sought to replicate in English most especially the humour and the underlying rhythm of the French text. With that aim uppermost I chose to introduce variations on the formulas where they worked best in English, not always in exactly the same place as in French. I also took some pleasure in using a word that is not attested in any dictionary that I can find but which was taught me by my Latin master, Jim Brogden. 'Circumperambulate' is a word of English spoken, heard and understood by pupils and teachers at Westcliff High four and more decades ago. It really should have been logged by a lexicographer by now.

David Bellos
Princeton, 10 October 2010

# the art and craft of approaching your head of department to submit a request for a raise

having carefully weighed the pros and cons you gird up your loins and make up your mind to go and see your head of department to ask for a raise so you go to see your head of department let us assume to keep things simple – for we must do our best to keep things simple – that his name is mr xavier that's to say mister or rather mr x so you go to see mr x it's one or t'other either mr x is at his desk or mr x is not at his desk if mr x is at his desk it will be quite straightforward but obviously mr x is not at his desk so all you can do is stand in the corridor waiting for him to come back or come in but let us suppose not that he never comes in that case there would be but one solution to go back to your own desk and wait for the afternoon or the morrow to launch your campaign afresh but as is often the case that he takes his time in which case all you can really do instead of walking up and down in the corridor is to go and see your colleague ms y whom we shall call henceforth ms wye to give a touch of human warmth to our schematic demonstration but it's one or t'other either ms wye is at her desk or ms wye is not at her desk if ms wye is at her desk it would be quite straightforward but let us suppose that ms wye is not at her desk in which case seeing as you have no desire to carry on walking up and down in the corridor while waiting for mr x either to return or to come in whichever may be the case the only course now available to you is to circumperambulate the various departments which taken together constitute the whole or part of the organisation of which you are an employee then go back to see mr x while hoping that this time he has indeed come back or in it's one or t'other either mr x is at his desk or mr x is not at his desk let us grant that he is not so you await his coming back or his coming in by walking up and down in the corridor sure but let's just suppose he's taking his time in this case you go and see if ms wye is at her desk it's one or t'other either she is in or she is not if she is not the best thing you can do is to circumperambulate the various departments which taken together constitute the whole or part of the organisation of which you are an employee but let's rather assume she is at her desk in this case it's one or t'other either ms wye is in a good mood or ms wye is not in a good mood let's suppose for starters that ms wye is not i mean really not in a good mood in this case you don't let it get you down and circumperambulate the various departments which taken together constitute the whole or part of the organisation of which you are an

• 5 •

employee then go back to see mr x hoping he has come in it's one or t'other either mr x is at his desk or mr x is not at his desk are *you* at your desk no so why expect mr x to be at his maybe he is at *your* desk expecting to give you a drubbing when you get back or maybe he is walking up and down in the corridor outside *his* boss's office that's mr zosthene whom we will henceforth designate as mr z so mr x is not at his desk and as a result you look out for his coming back or coming in while walking up and down in the corridor outside his office we grant without reservation that a certain length of time may elapse before mr x comes back or comes in we advise you that in order to cope with the boredom that your monotonous pacing could easily prompt you should go have a chinwag with your colleague ms wye provided of course not only that ms wye is at her desk if she is not you would not have much of a choice save to circumperambulate the various departments which taken together constitute the whole or part of the organisation of which you are an employee unless of course you were to go back to your own desk to wait for more auspicious times but also that she is in a good mood if ms wye is at her desk and in a bad mood circumperambulate the various departments which taken together constitute the whole or part of the organisation of which you are an employee but let us rather assume to keep things simple – for we must do our best to keep things simple – that ms wye is both in her office and a good mood in this case you enter ms wye's office and you have a chinwag with her at any rate it's one or t'other as time goes by either you spy mr x coming back or going in to his office or else you do not see mr x coming back or going in to his office let us assume the most likely outcome namely that you do not see mr x for the good reason that mr x does not come that is to say we are ruling out a hypothesis that would have been disastrous for our demonstration namely mr x coming back or going in without your noticing it from being engrossed in conversation with ms wye in this case you would have to carry on chatting with ms wye unless of course by misfortune your conversation had put ms wye in a bad mood if this latter circumstance had arisen you would have had no choice but to circumperambulate the various departments which taken together constitute the whole or part of the organisation of which you are an employee then wander back to your own desk lost in thought and awaiting happier days but in the end there has to be a moment while chatting with ms wye when you see mr x go past on his way in to or out of his office you must then act with speed and skill by finding a good excuse for getting out of ms wye's office otherwise you might ruffle her feathers and next time she won't even let you have a chinwag with her which would oblige you to circumperambulate the various departments which taken together constitute the whole or part of the organisation of which you are an employee in perambulations that would eventually become suspicious and maybe even annoy your head of department which is obviously not what you had in mind so you find a good excuse for getting out for example i have to pop out to feed the parking meter or i'm afraid i swallowed a fish bone at lunch or excuse me but i must go and have a vaccination against measles you go and see mr x with every reason to believe that since you just saw him going by mr x is now well and truly at his desk we shall suppose to keep things simple – for we must do our best to keep things simple – that mr x is indeed in his office although we should never forget as eugene ionesco once said that when there's a ring on the doorbell sometimes someone is there and sometimes not the truth lying somewhere between the two so mr x is in his office and as mr x is your line manager you knock before entering then await a response obviously it's one or t'other either mr x raises his eyes or mr x does not raise his eyes if he raises his eyes that means at least that he noticed your knocking and intends to respond to it either positively or negatively a mystery that will soon be solved by a decision that we could then subject to analysis but if he does not raise his eyes but carries on talking on the telephone reading his file refilling his fountain pen in short doing whatever he had been doing at the point when you knocked on his door that means either that he hasn't heard and yet i'm sure you knocked clearly and firmly or else that he doesn't want to hear in any case that comes to exactly the same thing from your point of view because if he has not heard your knocking it would be quite inappropriate and even unseemly to persist so if he does not raise his eyes you go back to your desk and decide to try your luck afresh in the afternoon or tomorrow or next tuesday or forty days later obviously when you do go back to see mr x he will have to be in his office if he is not then you would await his return in the corridor and if he were to be a long time coming you would go see ms wye and if ms wye were also not at her desk you would circumperambulate the various departments which taken together constitute the whole or part of the organisation which toys with you then you would go back to see mr x if he were still not there you would await him in the corridor or else go to see ms wye on condition not only that she be there but that she also happened to be in a good mood otherwise you would circumperambulate the various departments which taken together constitute the whole or part of the organisation of which you are an employee then you would go back to see mr x and if he were not in you would pace up and down in the corridor while waiting for him and if he were to be a long time coming you would go have a chinwag with ms wye until you espied mr x coming in or back to his office the simplicity of this conditional loop permitting us to imagine the hypothetical situation which is not really exceptional though relatively infrequent in which mr x is in his office at the moment you go to see him thus relieving you from waiting in the corridor from assessing whether or not ms wye is in her office from making the always unreliable judgement of ms wye's disposition and from circumperambulating the various departments which taken together constitute the whole or part of the organisation of which you are an exploitee so mr x is in his office and since mr x is your line manager you knock before entering then await his response obviously if there is no response you have no choice but to begin all over again so we shall go so far as to grant in our noble desire to keep things simple – for we must do our best to keep things simple – that by exceptional good fortune when you knock mr x who was indeed in his office really did raise his eyes and that definitely means that he heard you but does not mean at all that he wishes to see you right away in fact the wide range of signs and therefore of communicative intentions that can accompany his response may be divided into three main groups that call for three strategic responses on your part first by moving his head two or three times on the horizontal plane from right to left and left to right or else by a dagger-like glance that speaks volumes about his unwillingness to co-operate or by violently blurting out a verbal string he may indicate that he has no intention whatsoever of seeing you now or soon or ever but you are right to reckon this an unnecessarily pessimistic and frankly destructive hypothesis so we will not pursue it any further on the other hand it would be far too optimistic nay dim-witted to think that your head of department will by moving his bonce in the vertical plane up and down and down and up or else by issuing the most gracious smile will i repeat ask you to come in straight away in fact this hypothesis is so implausible so contradicted by quotidian reality that we shall reckon it being as impossible as the prior hypothesis and that obviously takes us to the third consisting of a message in articulate speech concocted for your exclusive use by your head of department serving to put things off by granting you the status of visitor at some unspecified and more or less distant future point in time let me put his cards on the table your head of department cannot or does not want to see you straight away but he has nothing against hearing what you have to say and he requests you most politely to be so kind as to accept an appointment to see him at 2:30 pm seeing as it is 9:30 am right now as i speak obviously you are not going to wait for the clock to strike the half of three in the corridor or in ms wye's office or in a circumperambulation of the various departments which taken together constitute the whole or part of the organisation of which you are an employee so you go back to your desk and reflect that it is indeed the case that your oh so magnanimous head of department has told you to come back at 2:30 pm you know that your head of department is a man of his word otherwise he would not be your line manager you know that he certainly does not use words lightly but you are sufficiently accustomed to the diciness of life not to mention the rubicons of existence to know full well that in the firm that pays your rent and bacon it sometimes doesn't take much for a line manager's mood to change despite his also being the nicest man in the world and that a given proposition uttered at half past nine may not be worth a penny come two-thirty if only because in the intervening lapse of time will arise the always crucial episode of lunch a ceremony whose more or less satisfactory outcome always has a more or less unfortunate impact on your interlocutor's inclinations thus you have every reason to glean what information you can on the staff cafeteria menu and to keep an eye on the dietary behaviour of your line manager during his midday meal several circumstances may obtain each of which requires an appropriate response from you so let us suppose that today is friday it's one or t'other either the cafeteria is serving an egg dish or it is serving a fish dish let us suppose the cafeteria is serving fish it's one or t'other either your line manager swallows a fish bone or your line manager does not swallow a fish bone let us suppose that your head of department who is also your line manager does swallow a fish bone in this case do not commit the almost fatal mistake of turning up at your head of department's office at 2:30 pm but wait until tomorrow which is not very practical as the day after friday is saturday and the office is closed on saturdays but this is a tricky issue we plan to cope with later on so we shall assume to keep things simple – for we must do our best to keep things simple – that your head of department likes eggs and we will posit that the problem of distinguishing between degrees of offness in eggs has been solved now let us also suppose that it is not friday there are many reasons why that is preferable the cafeteria is less likely to be serving fish or eggs and your head of department is less likely to swallow a fish bone or to get food poisoning from rotten eggs moreover if your head of department makes an appointment for the next day that next day cannot be a saturday which makes your task much easier but all the same do not make the mistake of believing that if it is not a friday the lunch problem can be set aside in fact we could easily be in lent in which case it's one or t'other either there was a fish dish for lunch or there was an egg dish for lunch if there had been fish either your head of department swallowed a fish bone or your head of department did not swallow a fish bone if he did not choke wait quietly until the afternoon if he did swallow a fish bone keep as calm as you can while waiting for the day after or even better wait until the end of lent we will not entertain the nonetheless quite plausible eventuality given your state of extreme agitation that *you* swallowed a fish bone that's something you would have to deal with on your own the best solution is to eat a piece of soft white bread it's a traditional remedy but it's proved invaluable over time just ask your head of department let us rather assume that eggs were on the menu

it's one or t'other either the eggs were off or
the eggs were not off if they were not off then
the red spots you can see on the face of your
head of department must have another cause
perhaps measles but if they were in such a state
of maturity (the eggs, i mean) as to give
grounds to fear that all who had the weakness
to consume them are now suffering an onset of
food poisoning and if your head of department
was one among such wait at least until the next
day unless it is really bad in which case you
have to wait either until the end of lent or for
your head of department to get over it
completely which could take a few days or
weeks or months or until his successor has been
appointed with which successor you proceed
in exactly the same way as with his predecessor
unless of course it turns out to be you hallelujah
who is chosen to take the place of your dearly
beloved head of department (deceased) and in
this case the issue of a raise will be far less acute

and you will wait for a few weeks months years before going to see your head of department or the chief executive of the firm of which you are an employee to make your desiderata quite clear do the art and craft of approaching a head of department or a chief executive to talk about an increase in your pecuniary emoluments have any relationship to the art and craft of approaching a line manager with the same objective that is a serious question that we can neither solve nor even realistically discuss in the light of the limited data currently available to us so we shall assume to keep things simple – for we must do our best to keep things simple – either that it is not a friday or a day in lent or that we are involved with a firm deeply committed to the secular ideal or that the cafeteria served filleted sole or fresh-laid eggs which all comes down to the plain-vanilla advice that we are giving you not to go and see your line manager on a friday or in lent so the lunch issue now being dealt with or so it seems does not arise you have no further qualms about the availability of your line manager unless of course it is monday if it is monday wait for tuesday you would have to be really stupid to go to see your line manager on a monday to talk about a raise as idiotic as going to see him on a friday afternoon or any afternoon in lent laying yourself open to having to deal with ticklish issues when face to face with an individual who instead of listening to you is wondering all the while whether the eggs he has just consumed really were fresh or if he had eaten enough soft white bread to ward off the potentially dire consequences of his having most unfortunately ingested a fish bone to sum up and between you and me it is never very wise to approach a line manager at a time when his gastric functions are likely to overshadow the professional and managerial capacities associated with his hierarchical rank it is far better to go see him in the morning but what the hell he himself told you to come and see him at 2:30 pm you have to take life as it comes so now it is 2:30 pm and you go to see mr x it's one or t'other either mr x is at his desk or mr x is not at his desk now you're going to say that since he told you to turn up at 2:30 pm he really ought to be in his office at 2:30 pm yeah yeah but that would be forgetting the twisted and sometimes even scoundrelly souls of hierarchical superiors mr x in order to impress upon you that he is your line manager may well tell you to come at half past two that is well within his rights and some would say his duties what are you going to do do not despair leave it to steep a while longer since mr x told you he would see you at 2:30 he will definitely be back soon so you should walk up and down in the corridor waiting for him to come and if he takes a while longer you will go and have a chinwag with ms wye on condition of course that ms wye is at her desk if ms wye is not at her desk you will circumperambulate the various departments which taken together constitute the whole or part of the organisation of which you are an employee or let's say an exploitee then you go back to try your luck anew a little later it is possible that even then mr x is not in his office no matter wait in the corridor then if he takes another while schmooze with ms wye do or die providing not only that ms wye is in her office but also a good mood otherwise you will have to circumperambulate the various departments which taken together constitute the whole or part of the organisation of which you are obviously not the brightest star while inwardly cursing your lord and master's bad faith but if on the other hand ms wye is in her office and her customary state of bonhomie you will be able to expatiate at lesser or greater length on the quality of the fish served at luncheon or the agedness of the eggs or just how difficult it is to pin down mr x oy vey that will be at least we hope so for your sake precisely the instant that you see him pass by mr x i mean and you will hasten to invent an acceptable pretext for example i have to pop out to feed the parking meter or i'm afraid i swallowed a fish bone or i wonder if the eggs weren't ex or you've got red spots on your face surely you haven't caught measles then you will go and knock on the door of mr x's office there is no good reason why he should not raise his eyes on hearing your taptaptap or not invite you to come in and to say what you have to say since in theory he himself asked you to come back at half past two and it's his own fault not yours if it is now well and truly three-twelve nonetheless we cannot be too careful to advise you or rather cannot advise you to be too careful and to consider the eventuality or rather eventualities that either he does not raise his eyes but that's to let you know that he cannot or will not his inability and unwillingness coming to exactly the same thing from your point of view see you or that he would very much like to see you but not now but only tomorrow morning or tomorrow afternoon at half past two yes such things do happen tomorrow is a friday you will be obliged to watch the cafeteria menu because if fish is on your line manager could easily swallow a fish bone and thereafter be in a really awful mood which will not be in your favour or else if by chance it is not fish eggs will be on and may be off and your line manager could easily get indigestion anyway even if it is not thursday today the day before friday tomorrow could be the first day of lent which would or easily could have the same unfortunate effect with respect to lunch and thus to your line manager's state of receptivity and he will surely hold it against you if you disturb him while he's querying the freshness of eggs or the future itinerary of the fish bone stuck in his oesophagus and even if tomorrow is neither a friday nor the first or any other day of lent do be careful not to choose a saturday because on saturdays your line manager does not come in to the office and nor do you that's actually one of the few perks available in the firm that works you or a sunday which is impossible because the day before sunday is saturday and on saturdays you don't go in to work or a monday which looks like a paradox but is not one because in the services sector the day after friday is monday if then your line manager tells you on friday morning to come back to see him on friday afternoon and if on friday afternoon he puts you off until monday morning not so much because he grudges the time he gives to you but because he swallowed a fish bone or because he has every reason to suspect that the eggs of which he took three helpings were ex and is therefore worried about them which you cannot but find legitimate tell yourself that on monday morning his disinclination to listen to your squalid concerns over pay will have even greater justification and it would be wiser when all's said and done to come back and try your luck again on tuesday morning or tuesday afternoon so let us suppose that you come back on tuesday morning clearly mr x is not at his desk nor is ms wye at hers with the result that you circumperambulate the various departments which taken together constitute the whole or part of the organisation which pays you to circumperambulate the various departments which taken together constitute the whole or part of one of the biggest firms in one of the key sectors of the nation's most national industries notwithstanding you return on tuesday afternoon your line manager is in his office you knock he raises his eyes he nods in the affirmative in short he tells you to come in all of which could be explained by the fact that at lunchtime the cafeteria served neither fish nor eggs but caviar and there's nothing like lumpfish roe to bring tears of joy to the eyes of your boss so obviously you go in since he told you to do so do not affect an air of disbelief abandon all rancour and refrain from observing to your head of department that seeing as you are now in his office he could bloody well have given you an appointment three weeks ago when having made up your mind to ask for a raise you had girded up your loins and come to knock on the door of his office where he happened not to be at that time forget all such things you have finally reached not the end of your road but at least the witching hour when you will soon be able to lay out the issue that concerns you it would be better to do it sitting down because it is tricky to pour your heart out standing up in front of even the most benevolent of line managers but as far as i can see you are still on your feet and you obviously cannot sit down until your line manager has invited you to do so explicitly well it's one or t'other either he asks you to be seated or he does not ask you to be seated if he asks you to take a pew and incidentally to relax everything could go if not swimmingly then at least in accordance with a process whose unfolding is fairly clear to you but what will you do if he does not ask you to sit down don't think this is such a rare occurrence don't assume that he has no respect or is ignoring you just because he leaves you on your own two feet that's not necessarily the reason it's much more likely he is beset by personal worries stick your neck out and ask him whether one of his daughters has perhaps caught measles he'll answer yes or no if he says yes one of his daughters has measles check discreetly this goes without saying whether or not he has red spots on his face if he has no spots breathe deeply relax and in an intelligible voice lay out your problem but if he has got spots on his face get out of there on any excuse for example i have to pop out to feed the parking meter or i'm afraid i swallowed a fish bone or i wonder if they weren't a bit off those eggs we got at lunch today or hang on i think ms wye is calling me inform health and safety and lock your boss in his office for forty business days that is to say for eight weeks after the eight weeks have elapsed go back to see your boss there's every likelihood he will be in his office but maybe he will refuse to see you in which case you will come back to try your luck a little later preferably in the morning and not on a monday or a friday or a day of lent remember that if mr x is not in his office when you go to ask for an appointment you can always wait for him by walking up and down in the corridor or if he is running late by schmoozing with ms wye if in fact she is in her office and a good mood or else by circumperambulating the various departments which taken together constitute the whole or part of the consortium which pays you a pittance while grinding away the best years of your life let us rather assume that everything goes to plan summoned by mr x at half past two on a wednesday you are in actual fact in his office the following tuesday on the stroke of ten he tells you to come in but he has not yet told you to sit down so you ask him whether one of his daughters has measles and he answers no don't believe it or rather do not believe that that means that none of his daughters has measles unless you have it on unimpeachable authority that mr x has only one daughter but it is much more likely he has four that's what it says on the flow-chart anyway and you can't invent this kind of thing so you ask him whether two of his daughters don't have measles he will answer yes or no if he says yes two of his daughters have measles you don't even have to squint up his nose to see whether or not he has red spots it's better to get out on some fabricated pretext for instance shit my meter or ouch a fish bone or again those eggs at lunch i wonder hang on i'm being asked for that must be ms wye who needs me for a T60 issue as soon as you are out the room rush to health and safety and have mr x locked in his office for the official incubation period that is to say forty business days once that period has elapsed go back and see mr x preferably on a tuesday or wednesday because it is obvious that if you go to see him on a thursday and he puts you off until friday you're going to have the lunch problem re fish and eggs on your plate and it's better to stack the chances in your own favour if perchance meanwhile mr x has managed to get out and has not yet come back in wait for him either by pacing up and down in the corridor or by nattering with ms wye unless ms wye has already retired and only if she is still suffused with the bonhomie of yesteryear or lastly by circumperambulating the various departments which taken together constitute the whole or part of the organisation with which you should definitely not identify yourself stick your neck out and check the lunch menu and get vaccinated against measles then with your heart full of hope go back to stand outside the office of mr x we shall assume to keep things simple – for we must do our best to keep things simple – that mr x is in his office that he raises his eyes when you knock and asks you to come in but still does not ask you to sit down so you ask him whether one of his daughters has measles he answers no whether two of his daughters have measles he answers no it's a good answer up to a point but it could be camouflage hiding a far worse truth namely that three of his daughters have measles put the question honestly if your line manager says yes three of his daughters have measles get out fast you don't even have to find an excuse alert health and safety and the first aid team have your boss locked in and the whole department to boot and even the departments on either side for forty business days and keep yourself in isolation as well in 1966 there were 18,931 registered cases of measles in france and 109 fatalities which gives you a pretty good chance with a survival rate of approximately 99.5% measles is an infectious disease of man marked by an eruption of rose-colored papulae in irregular circles and crescents that is to say by often acute facial efflorescence or exanthema it is preceded and accompanied by catarrhal and febrile symptoms typically sore throats sore eyes and coughing its principal complications are bronchial pneumonia laryngitis and encephalitis sulpha series drugs and penicillin provide effective medication it's better than catching scarlet fever forty days later you will still be able to go and see the firm's legal claims officer to request damages if the legal claims officer is not in you wait for him in the corridor or else you go and have a chinwag with ms jay providing she is in her office and a good mood or else you circumperambulate the various departments which taken together constitute the whole or part of the firm which defends the interests of the firm that employs you we shall consider despite the notoriously contagious nature of the above-mentioned disease that the simultaneous co-occurrence of three cases of measles in the same family is a sufficiently unusual event to impinge on the awareness of the head of aforementioned and your department and to lead him to take all necessary steps for the collective well-being of the firm of which he too is an employee and as a result it is likely that for once he will reply that no three of his daughters do not have measles sure but what is true of the three is not necessarily true of the four and it is well known that measles lies dormant the fourth offspring of your boss could well be nursing the infection whence the fatherly worries that cause him to forget even to offer you a seat so do worry about the health of the littl'un if the answer is that she gives some cause for concern wait for confirmation before acting if it really is measles it will soon be known and after all in the position you have reached you can't really claim that forty days more or less is here or there if on the other hand your line manager says that there is not the slightest risk of measles on the far horizon stop pushing the question you will end up arousing suspicion in the otherwise crystalline heart of your boss rather think that after completing all these sanitary routines you have more than adequately demonstrated your proper concern for the personal well-being of your head of department and for what he must hold dearest to be within your rights to sit down even before being explicitly invited so to do in other words either you behave as if when asked to come in you had also been asked to take a seat and so you sit down or while still on your feet you behave as if you were seated and begin to speak of the problem that is nagging at you so now you have got to the point we can indeed call crucial stop scratching relax breathe in remember nothing ventured nothing gained keep right on to the end of the road lay out your problem with honesty you know full well that what brings you here is a matter of money you earn 750 francs a month you would like to earn 7,500 you know it's going to be difficult you would settle for 785 plus an annual bonus pegged at the equivalent of 40 business days to compensate for incubation you also know that your line manager can see right through your little game and he knows why you're standing in front of him biting your nails pathologically stumbling over your words you know that he knows that you know and he knows you know that he knew that you saw that he would know that you were about to know in other words you have the actually quite accurate impression that it would be tricky clumsy dangerous to launch into the issue just like that you need a pretext you need to persuade your line manager that you deserve the raise for instance you are going to give him an idea that the firm to which you owe everything could use to its benefit you've been thinking about the international context competition is increasing with the dismantling of customs tariffs and the implementation of that accursed treaty of rome on the common market next month how will we sell anything expansion means you we're in this together lads there'll always be something left over the more we produce less fast the less we consume more slowly and vice versa et cetera but your line manager who sees what you're trying to do stops you by asking if this is a T60 issue it's one or t'other either it is a T60 issue or it is not a T60 issue but you haven't a clue what a T60 issue is and i can't help as i don't know either so you stick your neck out and obviously say yes this is a T60 issue but hang on your line manager exclaims with a burst of enormously sardonic laughter if it is a T60 issue then it doesn't come under me go and see AD 4 section for that is the only department that can deal with it all you can now do is to get up thank your head of department for the excellent advice he has given you and go and look for AD 4 section which obviously you will fail to locate while musing on your misfortune and swearing if somewhat belatedly that you'll never get caught out like that again you will wander from department to department then you will come back to see your head of department once again obviously your head of department will have to be in if he is not then wait in the corridor for him to turn up if he takes his time go and see ms wye if ms wye is indeed in her office and in addition in not too bad a mood but she is used to seeing you now so if she is there there is no good reason for her to shoo you away otherwise you would have to circumperambulate the various departments which taken together constitute the whole or part of the vast organisation where you are wasting the greater part of your time stick your neck out and ask around if someone else doesn't also have a T60 issue then drift back to mr x's office until such time as he is in which must eventually come to pass unless he got so ill from the eggs that were served yesterday but were not fresh or unless he has been laid low by ingurgitating a fish bone last lent or unless he is incubating a case of measles or unless he is himself pacing up and down in the corridor outside mr z's office that's his head of department to try to speak to him about a

U120 issue but let's suppose that all goes well that mr x is in you knock he doesn't answer such things do happen do not lose heart nor should you persevere that would be unseemly try your luck afresh the morning after except if the morning aforesaid falls on a monday or a friday or even a thursday because if you go to see him on a thursday and still he does not answer the knock on the door that puts you back not to the next day which would be a friday day of eggs and fish nor even to monday an unlucky day overcharged with magic memories of satsun but unto tuesday which is a long way off so all in all it's a better bet to decide right now to go to see your line manager on a tuesday because if he spurns you that still leaves all of wednesday to try your luck one more time so the following tuesday you go back to mr x's office and o joy o rapture he's there mr x is there he raises his eyes when you knock of course he can't see you but at least he summons you to come and see him that very afternoon at 2:30 pm if by good luck it is not lent then there's not much chance of fish or eggs being on the lunch menu and even if there are eggs they will not necessarily be off and if there is fish mr x is in no way obliged to swallow a bone in short you still have a good chance and on the very stroke of half past two you present yourself at the door of the office of your line manager who has no valid reason not to be there and yet such is the case you wait for him in the corridor then as he takes his time you go to see if ms wye is at her desk no she isn't so you circumperambulate the various departments which taken together constitute the whole or part of the tentacular organisation that provides your meagre means of subsistence on wednesday you clock in forthwith at your line manager's office let's suppose to keep things simple – for we must do our best to keep things simple otherwise we would be utterly lost — that he is in he being your head of department you knock he raises his eyes he beckons you to enter let's suppose he forgets to tell you to sit down but assures you that neither one nor two nor three of his daughters have measles and that his fourth-born isn't in the remotest danger of catching it recall that if this were not the case you would have to exit more or less precipitously depending on the seriousness of the situation alert health and safety or first aid or both at the same time lock your line manager in his office for forty business days with a supply of sulpha series medications and/or antibiotics and put yourself into isolation too but if despite forgetting to ask you to sit down while reassuring you that all his family are well then you have once again a small a tiny a minuscule a risible opportunity to achieve your ends of course you won't dare launch point blank into boss i wanna raise that would be clumsy you have to find a pretext without getting too tangled up so you undertake to explain to your line manager that as you are deeply concerned about the organisational equilibrium of the firm that is for you like a third teat and yet worried while also inspired by the recently remodelled competitive robustitude ipsified by the market how will we pay our suppliers next month expansion is other people industrial output is personal input and vice versa and so forth and so on it occurred to you that other things being if not equal scuse me is what your head of department will then say aren't we talking about a T60 issue it's one or t'other either we are talking about a T60 issue or we are not talking about a T60 issue since you still don't know what a T60 issue is you can say anything you like but you must not say yes because if you do your line manager will have it easy and be able to say that your thoughts touch him not a jot or tittle for they come under AD4 section or the dispatch department the disputes department the canteen health and safety first aid external relations ms wye or the legal claims officer and you would have to start all over again no for pity's sake no so you answer that it is definitely not a T60 harrumph harrumph harrumph your line manager will then say so we need to plan another project it's one or t'other either you lie and say yes or weary with all the lies you've told you say no pretty much forcing your line manager to be the first to utter the word raise let us suppose that in an attempt to outsmart the fates which you would be wrong to do but let's not get carried away too soon you said yes we need another project i'm listening your head of department will say so all you could then do is to lay out your proposal to your line manager of course the idea would have to catch your line manager's imagination let us suppose that it does not catch his imagination which is altogether the most likely situation have you ever seen a line manager get interested in an idea brought to him by one of his subordinates at best he will see in it an interesting suggestion he could hasten to suggest to his boss mr z as soon as the latter has fully recovered because after eating an omelette that his youngest daughter had lovingly cooked for him he caught measles so your head of department is going to pretend to find your proposal extremely dull boring and in addition totally impractical and to keep things simple he will ask you in a particularly icy tone to put it all down on one sheet of a4 which will go straight into the wpb all you can then do is exit do not lose heart after all you make a decent living do you really need a raise if you cut out the unnecessaries heating clothing transport if you have lunch in the canteen every day and dine on boiled lettuce you should be able to make both ends meet in any case it's a well known fact that boiled lettuce sharpens the mind and within a few months you get a non-trivial new idea that you reckon will fascinate your line manager and will allow you to drop a few hints about a hypothetical upward adjustment of your pecuniary emoluments so you go to see your head of department he is not at his desk you wait in the corridor but as he takes his time you go to see if ms wye is in her office she is but she greets you like a bullfrog in a pottery store so you circumperambulate the various departments which taken together constitute the whole or part of the firm that is your sole horizon then you go back to see mr x who is in his office he raises his eyes when you knock but gestures that he is busy and will see you on the morrow without fail at 2:30 pm alas the morrow is a thursday and mr x takes advantage of his daughters' day off school to take them to the clinic to have them vaccinated the next day is friday and you do not even try in any case you nearly choke to death on a fish bone and have no more than a quarter of your normal speaking voice left the following tuesday mr x leaves for his annual leave it's just a happenstance put it down to bad luck syndrome nothing you can do about it the day he gets back you catch measles then ms wye goes on her holidays then the economic situation constrains the firm to downsize quite seriously by a miracle you are spared which proves if proof were needed that you should never be overly pessimistic but it's not a good time to ask for a raise anyway it's lent then you have your annual leave when you get back you learn that mr x unsurprisingly swallowed a fish bone while eating eggs laid by hens raised on fish waste despite what you think all this is actually very helpful to you because when eight and a half months later you manage to corner mr x coming out of the cafeteria he will surely be very glad to see you and will ask you to drop by his office that very day at 2:30 pm so you go he will be there you will be seated as per his offer then following elementary courtesy you ask after his health and his loved ones and mme x is ok too and the four wee uns ah measles is a cruel disease measles cruel fate excuse me i've got some milk on the stove i must run without hesitation you present yourself at the door to the office of your head of department forty-one days later unless of course the forty-first day following this goes without saying is a thursday or a friday saturday sunday monday bank holiday the day after a bank holiday a day of lent or the eve of lent mr x now he's better will certainly be receptive to your request he might even see you on the spot and could go so far as to ask you to be seated relax breathe in lay out your problem no this is not a T60 issue do not make the horrendous mistake of saying so even if it is because your line manager will surely reply that T60s are not his potatoes and all you will then be able to do is to wander from department to department in search of potentially nonexistent experts in T60s say instead that you have another plan because if you start talking spondulicks straight away your line manager might find it fishy so you lay out your plan with all the ardour you can still muster it's one or t'other either your line manager will take an interest in what you tell him or he will not take an interest in what you tell him which is likely you will have wasted your time let us suppose as we are quite entitled to do that your head of department takes an interest in what you tell him it's not at all impossible at least in theory even if it has never actually occurred in recorded history so your line manager is taking an interest in your plan it's one or t'other either he thinks your idea is positive rich in possibilities worthwhile or he thinks it is stupid and will let you know in no uncertain terms that your logic is addled that's to say cock-eyed that's to say so devoid of understanding as to be close to either early-onset alzheimer's or congenital idiocy remember however that whether or not he calls you a nincompoop dimwit cretin nutcase crackpot woodenhead bananabrain dolt idiot or fool it comes to the same thing namely your plan will land in the wpb and you will return empty-handed to your desk while awaiting happier days it goes without saying that learning from experience you will improve your basic idea so when the day comes once again to talk with whole and open heart to your head of department he will be unable to dismiss you straight off as a nitwit so you allow yourself some months because one must always try to stack the odds in one's favour you swot up on the issue then when your plan seems perfect you go back to see mr x let's assume he's in and you don't have to wait for him in the corridor or go and have a bit of a chat with ms wye or even circumperambulate the various departments which taken together constitute the whole or part of the company in whose wheels you are at most a minuscule cog let us grant to keep things simple – for we must do our best to keep things simple – that by an even greater stroke of luck mr x answers asks you to come into his office and even goes so far as to ask you to be seated and tells you without prompting that his four daughters are in good health and married and that not one of his sixteen grandchildren seems at the present time to be incubating a case of measles he doesn't even ask you (your head of department that is) if the problem that brings you to him is or is not a T60 issue he seems very interested indeed in your plan it's even as if he finds your suggestion a fruitful one demonstrating a real capacity for observation critical thinking as astounding as it is instructive in short a really remarkable brain unfortunately he doesn't have time to give you a response don't be cross remember mr x must be overwhelmed that he spends all his time seeing or evading his twenty-four underlings your colleagues who like you appear to have one thing only on their minds namely to beg and whine for a raise which could in any case never be more than a paltry one and when through patient effort he succeeds in discouraging his subordinates for a few days he seizes the opportunity to go and see his own boss mr z who for his part never fails to put him off likewise his twelve colleagues without himself being able to get anything at all out of the assistant deputy deputy deputy director despite his harrying him without respite you have learned for every failure brings with it a lesson to ponder which will be of use to you later on you have learned I repeat that tenacity gets results and as you near the end of another campaign distinguishable from the others by mere minor details eggs not as fresh as they should be a fish bone that didn't go down properly measles afflicting the whole family there you are again face to face with mr x explaining that the use of office glue representing nought point nought three over ten to power three of the total cash flow of the business that you cherish more than anything else in the world could be cut by seventy-three point eight seven one per cent by the acquisition of an electronic glue dispenser that would be amortised in 760 weeks and could be paid for in monthly instalments all this seems to fascinate your line manager not stupid not stupid at all he says with a sly grin as a greedy glint lights up his eyes and his thick mop of brilliantined hair sparkles in the mauve glow of the setting summer sun then seemingly taking the time to answer you which constitutes a damn fine advance on where you got to last year he proposes to look at your problem more closely and before your very eyes starts going over the sums that led you to the conclusion that you got to by yourself and on your own now it's one or t'other when he's finished his sophisticated arithmetical task either your line manager will have understood the full meaning and import of your plan or he will not have understood a thing let's suppose he has not understood a thing it's somewhat disheartening but it's not really serious send your head of department to TV1 you don't know what a TV1 is nor does your head of department and neither do I let's say it's an information office an evening class a retraining scheme in short give your line manager a few weeks to let things sink in let's say a few months you must never try to rush things in theory it's up to mr x to let you know when he's finally grasped the point but you are well aware that he'll do nothing of the sort because otherwise he would not be your head of department would he so

you yourself after a respectable interval go back
to see him you will of course have to wait in
the corridor wait for him while chatting with
ms wye circumperambulate the various
departments which taken together constitute
the whole or part of the firm to which you owe
everything wait for the morrow wait for next
tuesday taste eggs spit wash out your mouth
petition the vatican to make lent and the eating
of fish on fridays fully optional wait for the
eldest of mr x's sixteen grandchildren to
recover but do not lose patience for there is a
strong chance that on your second or third
attempt your head of department will
understand but all the same don't go thinking
that all the rest will fall off a log for in actual fact
what has happened so far let us sum up let us be
clear you went to see mr x mr x was in you
knocked he raised his eyes and beckoned you
to come in he asked you to be seated you laid
out a plan which took his fancy he valued the

solutions you suggested he took time out to get to the bottom of your proposal and it now seems he has mastered it completely now that's all well and good but as of the present time you have not put in a single word about your indisputably justifiable claim for higher pay you could just about force yourself to grin to say er um as you wriggle on your seat but if mr x your line manager does not come out and offer you his congratulations how will you manage to tell him what the real problem is now as you surely know mr x is a line manager and a line manager never congratulates a subordinate so mr x never congratulates a subordinate and you are one of mr x's subordinates so mr x will never congratulate you and if mr x does not congratulate you you will not be able to talk about the raise and as he certainly won't bring it up himself all you will be able to do is to go back to your desk swearing if somewhat belatedly that you'll never get caught out like that again and next time you won't attempt to outsmart the fates but will utter right at the start the word raise and if it doesn't work so much for that well that's it you've made a wise decision so you go to see mr x your line manager he's not in his office and for a very good reason he's checking out the electronic glue dispenser so you circumperambulate the various departments which taken together constitute the whole or part of the vast organisation that is already using your electronic glue dispenser without moreover coming across a single soul that is explained by the fact that almost everybody is busy seeing how the electronic glue dispensing machine works or rather how it ought to work because it doesn't does it that electronic glue dispensing gizmo so you go to see for yourself how the bloody whatsit is behaving and you bump into your line manager who not only fails to congratulate you but on the contrary bawls at you you allow some weeks to pass allow his ire to subside then you go back to stand at the door of your superior he is not in you take a few steps in the corridor this way and that then go to see if ms wye is at her desk she is but seems disinclined to shoot the breeze because she's got an issue with her head of department mr wolfgang whom to keep things simple – for we must do our best to keep things simple – we shall obviously call mr w so morose and melancholic you circumperambulate the various departments which taken together constitute the whole or part of the organisation to which you feel proud to belong then go back to the office of mr x who blow me down is in who raises his eyes when you knock and even asks you with a charming smile to come in please take a seat and speak your mind that is so uncommon as to surely make you wary but as lucy van pelt says to charlie brown when she asks him to kick an american football that she will whisk out of range just as charlie brown thrusts his best foot forward at full speed thus causing him to fall which hurts more every time from the humiliation it engenders if you can't trust your bosses then you'll never get anywhere so you try out a shy smile you tell yourself that in principle mr x has nothing but the best of intentions in your regard and you confess that it is not a T60 issue that brings you that would not be of the slightest interest to him and would oblige you to wander lonely as a cloud in search of AD 4 section that you have not come with any other problem that might or might not be of interest to him and even if it were with a solution that might seem to him either fruitful or barren and even if he wanted to even if he appreciated your contribution he might or might not have the time to consider and even if he had the time to look at it carefully even if he set store by your proposal even if he were interested in the problem you are raising he might or might not understand and even if he understood appreciated took an interest in set store by was enthused by he could easily log your suggestion without thereby granting you the slightest laudatory remark or intent that would allow you to get down to the only topic which from your point of view is worth talking about to wit a substantial upward adjustment of your pecuniary emoluments so point blank looking at the whites of his eyes you boldly state that it is a matter of money ah ah ah says your line manager so you've come to see me about a raise say yes without a second thought first because it is the truth and you must always tell the truth second because if you say no your boss will have no trouble at all in asking you what the hell you are doing in his office at this hour instead of being in yours and at work in the service of the greater glory and good of the vast firm whose numerous departments that you circumperambulate with winsome fondness when your line manager is not in his office and ms wye is having a bad hair day constitute all or part you would have to hop it and god alone knows how kanga would ever find another opportunity to address him afresh face to face in his office your head of department's that is first of all he would have to be in it he would have to answer when you knocked at his door he would have to agree to see you right then or if he makes an appointment for the afternoon no culinary incident would have to impact on his bonhomie none of his daughters or grandchildren would have to be heading for a bout of measles so it's better to tell him the truth and to indicate to him that having been taken on at the age of sixteen years and three months as provisional assistant errand boy with a wage of 5,375 old francs and 50 old centimes a month you rose up the ranks step by step to your present position of assistant technical staff category 3 step 11 with a cost of living index rating of 247 which is to say real take-home pay after social security and other deductions in favour of the appropriate bodies of 691 new francs and 00 new centimes if your line manager is crafty and he is or else he would not be your line manager he will observe that you are certainly not working ten times as much as at the time of your first hiring and yet you are earning ten times more and he can't see what you are grumbling about i'm not asking for myself you will say sir but for my poor children my four wee girls who have just caught measles this last piece of information may perhaps not constitute a real argument in favour of your nonetheless quite justifiable claim all things considered it would be better to leave it out next time all the more so because next time your four wee girls not to mention you yourself will surely have got over it thanks to antibiotics and sulpha series medications to be found in great abundance among the range of pharmaceuticals available in france which are moreover refundable by the national health insurance scheme for which you pay regular premiums so once you are out of the sickbay you weigh the pros and cons you go to see mr x let us suppose to keep things simple – for we must do our best to keep things simple – that it all goes swimmingly let me check for the record that a fully favourable conduct of the campaign requires the beneficent and therefore inherently unlikely concordance of a heap of items variously located in the animal vegetable and mineral domains among them we will mention only – because we really do want to keep our demonstration as short as possible and not burden it with matters that would in the end be considered otiose – so among them we will mention I repeat only the good mood of ms wye the freshness of eggs the line manager's oesophagal unobstruction the absence of measles these conditions being met we can more easily grant that your head of department may see you and not have a priori reasons for dismissing out of hand your request for a raise does he not himself spend his time trying to get one from mr z all the same it's a well-known fact that no line manager ever grants a raise or even considers such a matter with even an iota of seriousness without having first gone right through the claimant's own view of the admissibility of said wish now obviously if you had a good idea which would allow the business that has always placed its trust in you to cut its wage base by 40% while increasing its profits by the same amount that would perhaps count in your favour but I seem to remember we have proven scientifically that you cannot have any ideas of the sort because either you have T60 ideas that are of no interest to anybody or else you think you have an idea but either your line manager could not give a damn or does give a damn but finds it too stupid or does give a damn and does not find it too stupid but doesn't have the time to think about it your idea I mean or does give a damn does not find it too stupid does have the time to think about it but can't make head or tail of it or else does give a damn does find it brilliant finds the time to take it on board and understands it from head to tail your idea that is but forgets meanwhile that you had come to see him about a raise so it is far better not to have an idea the part you played in a major project carried out by your firm with great brilliance could give significant support to your request for pecuniary enhancement you will be asked frankly answer in like manner if you have recently been involved in a successful project say yes if you have not been involved in a major project say no if you have recently been involved in a major cock-up say nothing about it and if you were involved long long ago in a very minor project which though not exactly a disaster could not be counted a real success say nothing about that either obviously it could be the case that your company has pulled off a number of major coups but that those were the ones in which you were not involved or worse still that it inexplicably bungled all the projects in which you played a major or minor part do not draw hasty conclusions and in any case to keep things simple – for we must do our best to keep things simple – we will not take such eventualities into account but let us suppose for this is indeed the most likely situation that you have not been involved in a recent major successful project which can be accounted for by the fact that your firm hasn't carried off a major coup for nearly four years now not for lack of wanting but its attempts to establish a shipyard in chartres a rail link from dunkirk to tamanrasset or to build a medical centre in the paris region all turned out to be unviable so you answer that you have not recently been involved in a major successful project do not add there is no point that you did all you could your line manager knows that and that is the very reason he holds you in such esteem moreover do not think all is lost all is not yet lost if you keep on good terms with your engineer that could stand in your favour and so your line manager solely in order to help you will ask if you are on good terms with your engineer answer as honestly as you can if you are on good terms with your engineer say yes if you are not on good terms with your engineer say er let us suppose that you are not on good terms with your engineer such things do happen you have nothing against him personally but he gets on your nerves and what's more he spends his time getting at you for not being at your desk or for getting in late he keeps on asking where you've been after all it's not your fault if mr x is never at his desk when you go to see him after having weighed the pros and cons and girded up your loins to ask for a raise of course it is not necessary to inform mr x of all the bones you have to pick with your engineer because mr x for strictly professional reasons discipline being the solid foundation of all firms be they in the national nationalised or private sector could take your engineer's side so restrain yourself from uttering more than er or perhaps um sigh if you have to hold down your tears pull out a few of your hairs strike your breast but above all do not attempt to tell a real whopper that would not be any use because mr x will in any case take advisement from said engineer and that will be worse tell yourself that even engineers do not live for ever that he may yield to the temptations of the brain drain that he may choke on a fish bone or get food poisoning from an egg that is off or succumb to complications arising from late-onset measles you do not even have to give fate a helping hand or if you do get it done without any witnesses around leave no clues and cook up a cast-iron alibi so we shall suppose to keep things simple – for we must do our best to keep things simple – either that fate has been extremely kind to you or that you did not get caught in short here you are with a new engineer get on with him for instance by pretending to get on with the job or why not by actually doing the job for a few weeks you'll see it can be quite interesting anyway it's no bad thing for you to give up the habit of going to see mr x every five minutes at least for a while mr x is beginning to get a bad impression when after a few weeks or a few months the air has been cleared you are getting on with your new engineer like a house on fire the criminal investigation department has given up on the case charges against mr x have been dismissed the company got a major government subsidy that saved it from going broke you turn up once again to see mr x he's not in no matter you pace up and down in the corridor while you wait then since he seems to be a long time coming you go to see if you can have a schmooze with ms wye but ms wye is not in her office and it doesn't seem she's in a good mood either so you circumperambulate the various departments which taken together constitute the whole or part of the organisation which has given you everything and if you bump into your engineer grace him with your most gracious smile but don't forget that next time you should be equipped with some file or other to justify your being in the vicinity of a department you have nothing to do with in theory nor does your engineer by the way but pointing that out to him won't get you very far some days later go back to see mr x he is still not in you wait in the corridor then you go to see ms wye but ms wye though appearing to be in the very best of moods is not in her office and so you gear yourself up to circumperambulate the various departments which taken together constitute the whole or part of the huge organisation in whose bosom you are bored stiff for forty-five hours a week when you see mr x appear at the end of the corridor so five minutes after you go and knock on his door but naturally he doesn't even answer and you return downcast but not really disheartened for it takes more than that to knock you down to your desk you do not try your luck anew the next day because the morrow is thursday and if mr x were to put you off to the day after the morrow that morrow would be a friday and mr x might scratch himself on a fish bone or get indigestion from none-too-fresh-laid eggs and in the situation that is now yours with two years and three months still to go before retirement it has become dangerous to take unnecessary risks you wait until the following tuesday which proves to be a happy day since you find ms wye at her desk at your first attempt and delighted to have a chitchat on the other hand you don't see a sign of mr x and as your conversation peters out after three hours and fifteen minutes ms wye having lost all her good humour throws you out and asks you not to come back tomorrow wednesday you quite pointlessly circumperambulate forty-five times in a row the various departments which taken together constitute the whole or part of the vast organisation where you eat your heart out the next day thursday you avoid meeting mr x altogether but in the ardent wish to stack all the odds in your favour you produce a weighty tome of paperwork for your engineer who deigns to say thank you the following day friday you clumsily knock the contents to wit a seafood salad and a portion of baked alaska off your cafeteria tray thereby soiling the freshly-pressed suit of your line manager mr x out of caution you allow two weeks to pass before making any new attempt then you go to see mr x but mr x is not in so you wait for him in the corridor then as ms wye seems to be still in a foul mood you circumperambulate the various departments which taken together constitute the whole or part of one of france's most powerful concerns then you go to see mr x he is in he raises his eyes when you knock he tells you to come in and even asks you to be seated despite having lots of little red spots on his face but as you've been taught that you must only ask your line manager if one of his daughters has measles if he fails to offer you a seat you do not ask him about his health or the health of his loved ones you try to relax and to lay out your problem well let's see says mr x is this a T60 issue no you say does this involve another project no you say is this about a raise yeeees you blurt now let's see your line manager then says have you recently been involved in a major successful company project not really you say ah ah says mr x are you on good terms with your engineer yeees you blurt in triumph well and good says mr x and what can we do for you you see it's all gone swimmingly no major incident has inflected the straight path of your two hundred and fifty-fifth bid could it be at long last that after so many years devoted persistently to this sole project you are at long last nearing your goal i really don't think so myself but that's not a reason for you to disbelieve in clear and intelligible speech smiling through your tears restraining the emotions that well up from your heart you explain that you earn 691 francs a month and would like to er um earn er perhaps not 6,910 or even 6,190 or even 1,960 or even 1,690 but er 961 or 900 well 850 er 800 ok 791 take it or leave it all right i'll come down to er 700 fine says your line manager do not make the naive mistake of thinking that your line manager will answer with a yes or with a no rest assured you will not get the raise you want I mean you will not get it in the here and now just like that on the nail you will not leave the office of mr x richer by 9 francs a month you have to grasp that in a company such as the one you work for one of the largest major companies in france a raise raises very complex issues not only with respect to accountancy but with respect to all aspects of the socio-economic policies for the short medium and long term of said company moreover it is obvious that mr x does not have the power to give you a raise just like that by clicking his fingers the most he could do is write a letter of support to the head of human resources who after consulting the appropriate authorities could propose as a part of an overall recalibration of the wages component of the company's outgoings a recalibration intimated moreover in the fifth national economic plan to put forward your name to an upcoming meeting or one of the subsequent meetings of the board of directors to sum up mr x though unable to meet your request on the spot can either give you to understand that your initiative not only does not surprise him but makes him wonder why you have taken so long to come up with it because he has always been in favour of such a step and encourages you to cherish the hope of promotion in a not excessively distant future time or tell you more or less straight out that he finds your demands unjustifiable cynical base and mean and that he never imagined you supposedly a model employee capable of such skulduggery in short either he gives you grounds for hope or he does not let us suppose he does not you now have several options for instance you could allow yourself to be seduced by pastures new and apply for a job with a rival firm but don't forget that with eighteen months to go before retirement you won't get many stellar offers alternatively you could go in for kidnapping blackmail or falsifying accounts but don't forget that these three avocations apart from requiring considerable skill are severely punished by local courts you could also sell the closely guarded manufacturing secrets that your firm keeps in a safe under lock and key to the highest bidder but to do that you would have to know what they are you could also bet on the horses but you already do bet on horses in short the best thing in my view is still to let it ride for another six months then go back to see your line manager we shall suppose to keep things simple – for we must do our best to keep things simple even at this stage of the game – that this fresh approach will not take any more time than any of your previous approaches it could perhaps take even take less time if with all the wisdom you have gleaned from experience you learn to stack all the odds in your favour you must not be an out-and-out pessimist you mustn't always look only on the dark side mr is x is not a bad sort the powerful firm you work for is not intent on giving you only grief your engineer has no reason not to get on with you bone-free fish also exist eggs are not always off if it is caught in time measles is not a serious illness and nothing prompts us to believe that the next time you are seated face to face with mr x and telling him all the ins and outs in a now slightly quavery from advancing years voice of your difficult existence and existential difficulties he will not listen with attentiveness sympathy nay real emotion and not allow you to glimpse the possibility of a not too distant raise you really shouldn't hold it against him if the raise doesn't arrive in the days immediately following we explained at some length that it was a complicated issue wait for six months then when six months later your hopes have been fully dashed go back to see

• 79 •

mr x if he is there if he raises his eyes when you knock if he asks you in straight off if he asks you to be seated and agrees to hear you out try to persuade him just one more time.

Printed in the United States
by Baker & Taylor Publisher Services